My Groundhogs
By Louise Blaker

Illustrated by Kathryn Howl

Uncle Dave's Books

3476 Douglas dr.

Murrysville, Pa 15668

www.uncledavesbooks.com

I live in Pennsylvania where groundhogs tend to gather. There are even famous ones that are said to predict the weather.

I want to tell you about my groundhogs.
They were so cute and furry.
They made me smile most everyday.
Here is my little story.

I had a groundhog in my backyard.
She had a little baby.
I named the groundhog Gertrude.
I named the baby Sadie.

They lived under the shed,
that we used to store the tools.
They came out when the sun was
bright,
and when the rain made pools.

I loved to watch them run and play.
They were not afraid of me.
I'd sit on the porch for hours,
their antics fun to see.

On days when it was very hot
and a tiny breeze came by,
they'd stand and raise their
arms to cool their underside.

**The groundhogs liked to eat the apples
from a tree that's in the yard.
They always stood to eat them
the cores they then discard.**

**Vegetables from the garden,
they sometimes tried to steal.
The fence only slowed them down,
because they wanted a meal.**

**Groundhogs love zucchini and melons
beans, peppers, and tomatoes.
Their hands are good for digging
so they even get potatoes.**

Mom and dad wanted them to leave the garden. So they'd run about and shout. Gertrude and Sadie left for awhile but noise didn't keep them out.

**Some people I have heard
have groundhog pie for lunch.
But I could never eat them,
on a friend I could not munch.**

**I would have been happy
if you could have visited me.
We could have watched the groundhogs,
they were better than T.V.**

The neighbors liked the groundhogs
For as long as I could remember,
then a new woman moved next door
early in December.
When I first saw her she looked as
pretty as could be,
but she said in a very mean voice
"Stay off my property"!

When spring arrived I was in the yard, and much to my delight six groundhogs two large and four small Burst into my site.

Gertrude and Sadie each had twin babies.
They were so cute and furry.
My dad said "I'll reinforce the garden fence, and do it in a hurry"!

I watched the groundhog babies grow.
I watched them run and play.
My Dad brought them apples from the
store because they ate all day.

One day they ate our neighbors' plants and I heard her say "I'll call animal control to take them away!"

Animal control set a trap on her property. I hoped the groundhogs would not go near, but Gertrude was caught on the second day. I couldn't help but shed a tear.

Animal control came to take Gertrude away. My mother said "OH, no"! We followed the man in the car to see where he would go.

**He went to the wooded area
with grass and a stream.
Gertrude ran out of the trap.
The place was a groundhog's dream.**

I don't know what happened to the others. I see one groundhog now and then. It's a shame our neighbor couldn't share her plants with them.

I hope I see a groundhog next year.
I hope she has a little baby.
I'll name the groundhog Gertrude
I'll name the baby Sadie.

Made in the USA
Middletown, DE
19 April 2019